Tickety
Tock

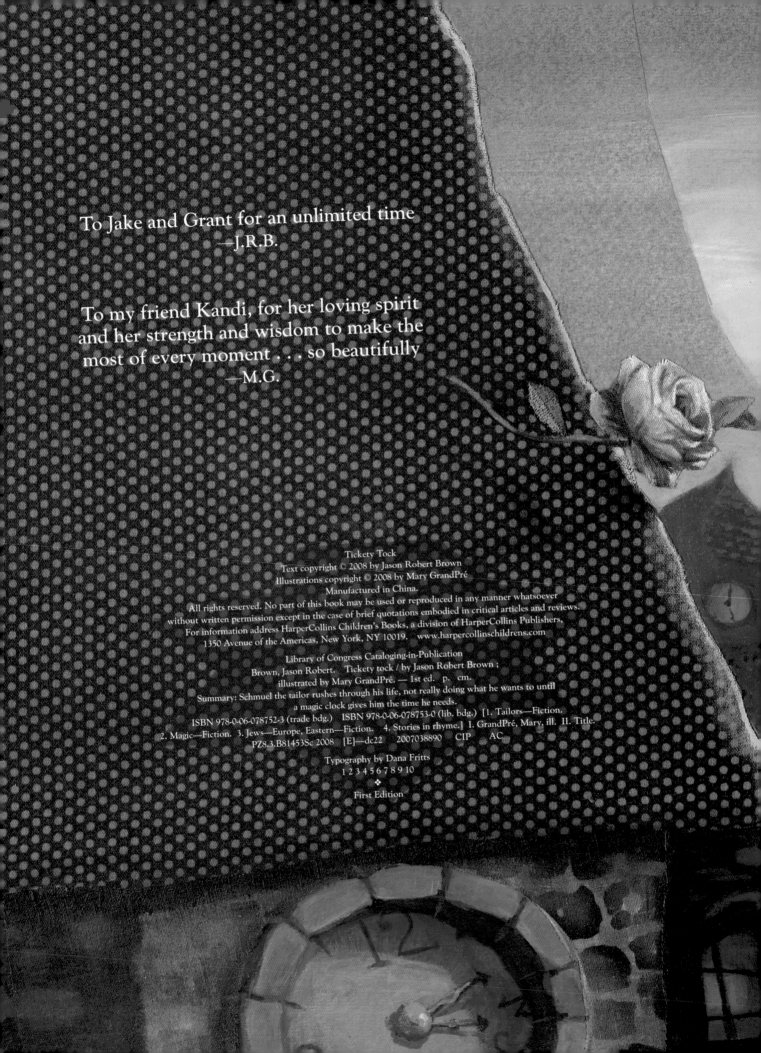

To Jake and Grant for an unlimited time
—J.R.B.

To my friend Kandi, for her loving spirit
and her strength and wisdom to make the
most of every moment . . . so beautifully
—M.G.

Tickety Tock
Text copyright © 2008 by Jason Robert Brown
Illustrations copyright © 2008 by Mary GrandPré
Manufactured in China.

For information address HarperCollins Children's Books, a division of HarperCollins Publishers,
1350 Avenue of the Americas, New York, NY 10019.  www.harpercollinschildrens.com

Library of Congress Cataloging-in-Publication
Brown, Jason Robert.   Tickety tock / by Jason Robert Brown ;
illustrated by Mary GrandPré. — 1st ed.   p.   cm.
Summary: Schmuel the tailor rushes through his life, not really doing what he wants to until
a magic clock gives him the time he needs.
ISBN 978-0-06-078752-3 (trade bdg.)   ISBN 978-0-06-078753-0 (lib. bdg.)   [1. Tailors—Fiction.
2. Magic—Fiction.  3. Jews—Europe, Eastern—Fiction.  4. Stories in rhyme.] I. GrandPré, Mary, ill.  II. Title.
PZ8.3.B81453Sc 2008   [E]—dc22   2007038890   CIP   AC

Typography by Dana Fritts
1 2 3 4 5 6 7 8 9 10
❖
First Edition

# Tickety Tock

By
Jason Robert Brown

Illustrated by
Mary GrandPré

LAURA GERINGER BOOKS
*An Imprint of HarperCollinsPublishers*

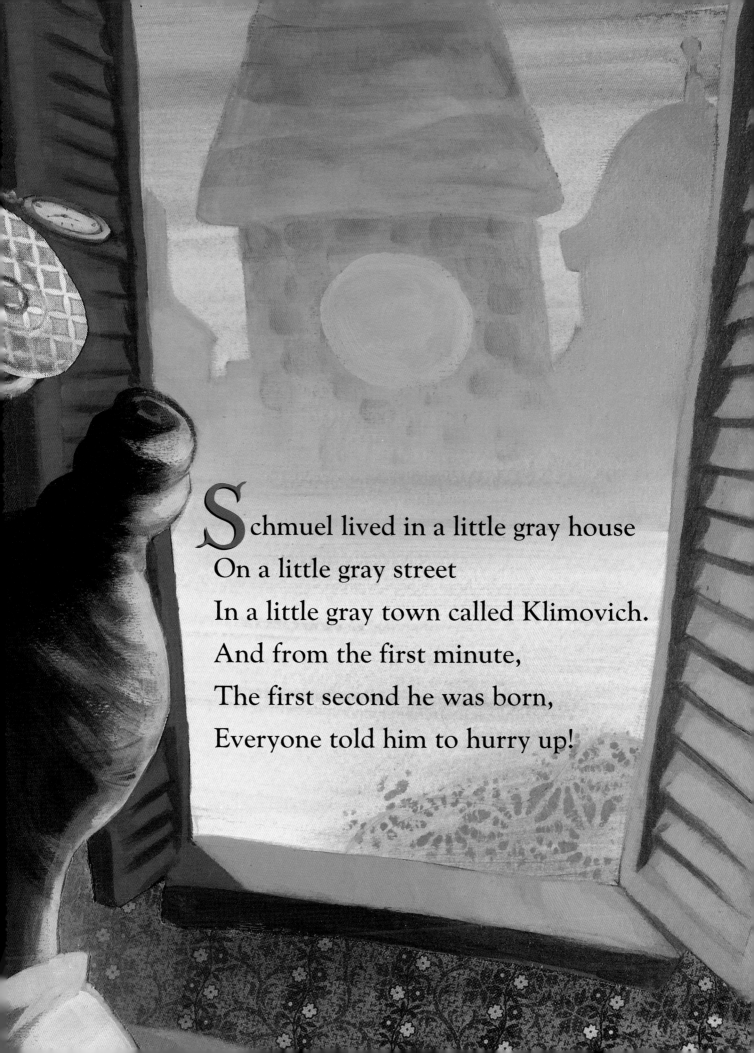

Schmuel lived in a little gray house
On a little gray street
In a little gray town called Klimovich.
And from the first minute,
The first second he was born,
Everyone told him to hurry up!

"Why isn't he walking yet?"
And then, when he could walk:
"Why isn't he talking yet?"
And then, when he could talk:
"There are chickens to feed and floors to scrub!"
"Get out of that bed!"
"Don't stay in that tub!"
"There are lessons to learn
And trades to master!"
"Faster, Schmuel! Faster!"

Schmuel's father taught him to sew
And showed him each stitch a good tailor should know.
He said to him, "Work is what helps you to grow,
So don't stop until that old clock says so!"

Then a girl at school
Said to him, "Schmuel!
Won't you make a dress for me?
As white as a swan,
As blue as the sea!
And put flowers and leaves
All over the sleeves!"

"I'm sorry," said Schmuel. "I have to run.
There are so many things I have to get done!"

But she chased him and yelled, "Don't forget to design
A little red heart to go right over mine!"

A day would come, a week would pass,
A month would turn, a year would fly,
And time rushed all too quickly by.

Schmuel would work 'til half past ten
At his tailor shop in Klimovich,
Get up at dawn, and start again
With the hems and pins and twist.
Forty-one years he worked alone
At his tailor shop in Klimovich.
All of those years he'd stitched and sewn,
There was one thing Schmuel missed.

"If I only had time," old Schmuel said,
"I would build the dress that's in my head,
As blue as the sea, as white as a swan,
With feathers and petals stitched perfectly on,
But I have no more hours left to sew."

Then an old clock upon the wall began to glow . . .

And the clock said:
"Tickety-tock tick!
Schmuel, you'll get to be happy!
Tockety-tick tock!
I give you all the time you need!
Tickety-tock tick!
So Schmuel, go sew and be happy!"

Old Schmuel said, "No, it's much too late.
I'm at peace with life, I accept my fate. . . ."
But the clock said, "Schmuel!
One stitch and you will
Unlock the dreams you've lost!"

So Schmuel grumbled and grabbed his thread,
Some bolts of velvet and silk, and he said:
"I should go home and go to bed.
I'm wasting time
With talking clocks instead!"

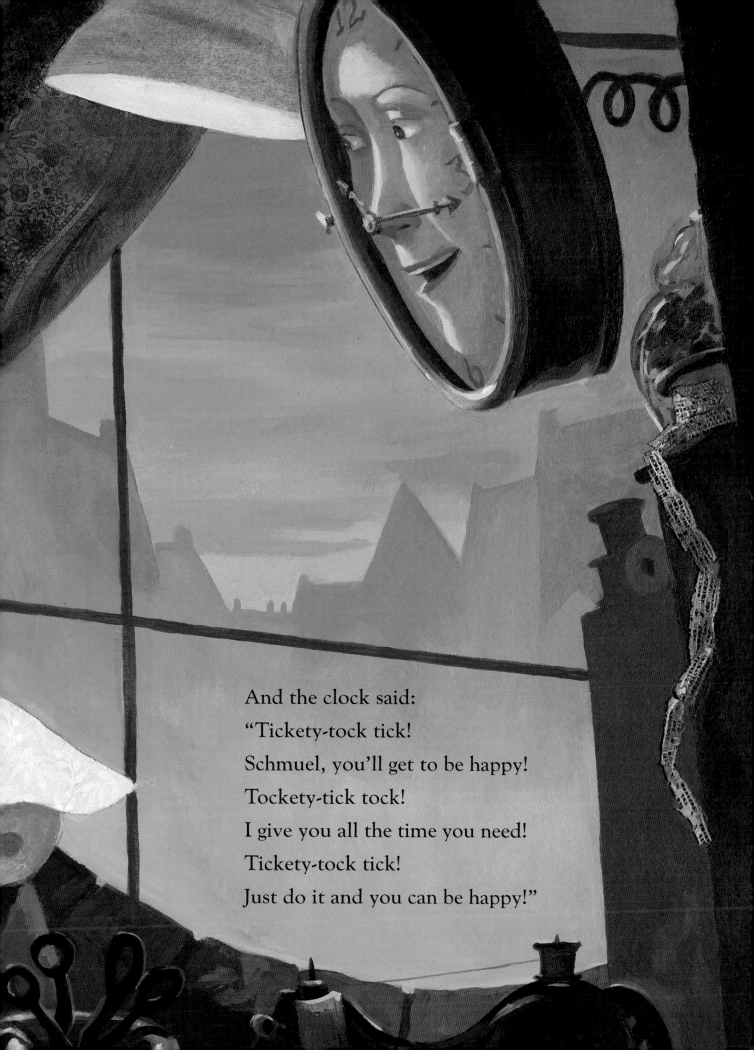

And the clock said:
"Tickety-tock tick!
Schmuel, you'll get to be happy!
Tockety-tick tock!
I give you all the time you need!
Tickety-tock tick!
Just do it and you can be happy!"

So Schmuel put the thread through the needle's eye,

And the moon stared down from a starless sky.

And as he pushed the thread through the velvet, he found

That his knees were shaking

And his stomach was churning—

For the hands on the clock had started turning

The wrong way around!

So he grabbed his shears and he cut some lace
As the hands reversed on the old clock's face!
And his fingers flew and the fabric swirled—
It was nine fifteen all around the world!

Every cut and stitch was a perfect fit,
As if some strange fate was controlling it!
And Schmuel cried, through a rush of tears,
"Take me back!
Take me back all forty-one years!"

And on it went, down that silent street,
'Til Schmuel's dress was at last complete,
And he stretched his arms, and he closed his eyes,
And the morning sun finally started to rise.

And the dress he made on that endless night
Was a dress that would make any soul take flight!
It was blue as the sky
And white as snow,
And the collar was loose
And the hem was low.
There were flowers and leaves
All over the sleeves,
And a tiny heart, stitched
Where a real heart would go.
And sewn into the seams
Were forty-one seasons of dreams.

And that very dress, so the papers swore,
Was the dress a girl in Odessa wore
On the day she promised forevermore
To love a young man
Named Schmuel
Who only one day before
Had knocked at her kitchen door.

Was that young man named Schmuel
The Schmuel we knew,
Who rushed and pushed and hurried
His entire life through?
And if it was our friend Schmuel,
How'd he pull off that trick?

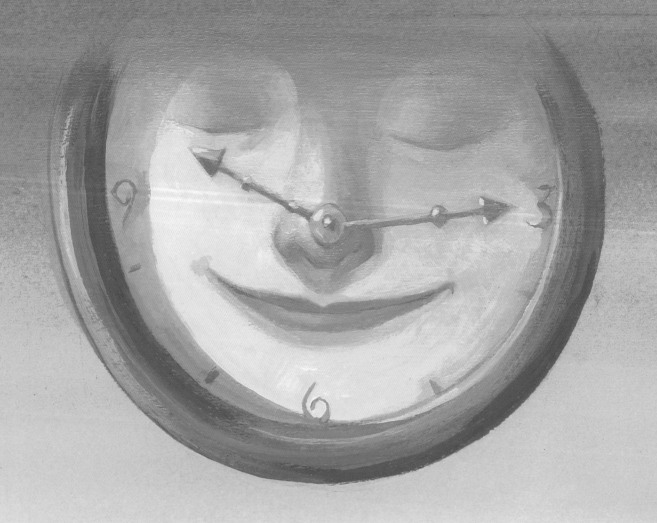

Tickety-tock.

Tockety-tick.